I0784683

Dedication

To my loving wife,

Natasha Marie Potter,

Thank you for always believing in me, even on the days when I doubted myself. Your support, your patience, and your unwavering love have carried me through every chapter of my life. You encouraged me when the pages were blank, stood by me when the story grew heavy, and reminded me that every dream is worth pursuing.

This book exists because of the support you have given me.

For that, and for so much more, I dedicate this story to you.

With love,

Your loving husband.

Acknowledgement

I would like to express my heartfelt gratitude to everyone who contributed to the making of this novel. To the individuals who offered their time, talent, and dedication, thank you. Your support has been invaluable throughout this journey.

To all the authors whose work has inspired me over the years, your insight, imagination, and dedication helped shape this story more than you will ever know.

To my friend Robert justice who encouraged me along the way, your belief in my work gave me the strength to keep writing.

To my mother, Kandis Barrow, whose love for storytelling lit the spark that grew into a passion for Gothic writing. Without her early influence and the world she opened for me, this book would never have existed in the first place. Thank you, Mom, for planting the love of stories in my heart.

And to everyone who offered guidance, inspiration, or encouragement, I am grateful to each and every one of you. This novel exists because of the many hands and hearts that supported it.

Thank you for being part of this creative path. May each page you read carry the same passion and heart that went into writing it!

Table of Contents

Chapter 1

On the darkest of nights, Tony is barely running and mostly limping as he's bleeding out, bursting through the double doors with a desperate force, leaving a trail of blood behind him. He charges down the long hospital hallway, his legs trembling under the weight of pain, every muscle aching as fear wraps itself around him like a shadow on a cold, gloomy day.

Senses so alert he could hear the ticking of the analogue clock on the wall echo sharply as he passed by, each second stabbing at his nerves and reminding him that time was slipping through the gaps of his fingers. With tears coming out of his eyes, blurring his vision, Tony pushes past the excruciating pain, dragging himself forward with sheer will, hoping against despair as he fights to reach his family; if anything happens to them, he knows he will never forgive himself; the thought constantly circling in his mind.

After what feels like an eternity, Tony reaches the room at the very end of the hallway, the door slightly cracked open, waiting for him like the final breath before a storm. He rushes inside.

Once Tony saw his would-be killer, he did not hesitate to bum-rush the man dressed in black. This murderer was pointing a gun at a shadowy figure who stood protectively over two smaller shadowy figures, shielding them with their body. Just before the hunter could take out his prey, Tony transforms from a ruggedly handsome Caucasian male with dark short-cut hair and turquoise eyes, into a vicious looking werewolf: wild, matted brunette fur that bristled with every breath, and bright yellow eyes that glowed like feral embers; a low growl vibrating from deep within his chest.

The man in black witnesses every second of the transformation, the air thickening around them, filled with a low rumble as bones shift beneath Tony's skin. Just before the hunter gets the chance to pull the trigger on the shadowy figures, he desperately redirects his attention and fires the silver bullet straight at Tony, only this time, instead of the silver bullet passing through Tony's body like the last one, it lodges deep into his lungs with a wet, heavy impact. But with his natural adrenaline surging through him, Tony manages to sink his teeth and claws into the hunter as he rushes forward, the metallic scent of blood hitting the air as the two of them slide violently across the floor together, crashing straight through the glass wall directly across from the room's entrance. Both plunge six stories straight down; the shadowy figures watching all of this in complete, utter shock. For a second, there was complete silence; however, moments later, a haunting, sorrowful howling rose into the night air as if wolves were mourning the loss of a loved one.

That scream, that fall, became the sound that never leaves Sharon Richards. Though some time has passed since that awful night, every day feels like the same story. Sharon wakes from another nightmare, reliving the moment her loved one died; a memory that continues to haunt both her dreams and her days.

She's dripping with sweat from the night terrors, breathing heavily as she tries to calm herself. She does her best to remain focused, reminding herself that some things are beyond our control and that dwelling on the past will only keep her from embracing a future with hope. Sharon places her hands palms down on her lap and concentrates on her breathing, taking slow, steady exhales as she counts each breath.

She works to bring her emotions from a boiling panic to a gentle simmer, feeling the air move in and out of her body as she gradually regains a sense of control and the ability to relax. Once a faint comfort settles over her from the breathing exercises, far better than how she felt when she jolted awake, Sharon gets out of bed and takes a shower to complete her exercise in self-control. After the shower, Sharon goes to her favorite bookstore in town, Mr. Lee's book shop.

She walked inside, just as she always does, and said, *"Hello, Mr. Lee, how are you on this fine day?"* Joyful as ever.

"I'm well, Sharon, so how many books will it be today? I do have some new ones." He asked.

"Okay, sounds interesting, I'm listening." Sharon, curious.

"Well, you do love a good romance, and I have a lot of romantic novels from your favorite author, Heidi Combs." Mr. Lee informs her enthusiastically.

"Oh, wow, you know me, don't you, Mr. Lee?" Sharon impressed.

"If I don't know my customers, I shouldn't be in business," Mr. Lee makes clear.

"I agree," Sharon said, smiling.

"Here they are, all seven of Heidi Combs' romance novel saga My Bloody Tears." Mr. Lee told her and continued, *"I saved them just for you."*

He shows clear satisfaction as he presents the gifts, the stack of books cradled in his hands like treasured finds.

"Oh, thank you so much, Mr. Lee." Sharon shares her appreciation; her voice softening as she grows a little teary-eyed.

"My pleasure, Sharon, no problem at all," he replies, giving off his unique, tailored customer service warmth.

Storming into the entrance is a young boy, followed closely by his little sister, their hurried footsteps pattering across the floor as their mother chases after them.

"Slow down, you two! I mean it!" she calls out, very stern with her kids.

"Good morning, Monica," says Sharon as she clutches her books.

"I got you, you're it," the young girl says.

"Yeah, whatever, you're still too slow, Puppy...," says the boy.

Just before he could finish taunting his little sister, Monica interjects, *"Now that's quite enough, Zack, shut it,"* then looks over to Sharon and politely adds, *"Good morning, Sharon!"*

"I see you got your hands full," Sharon replies.

"When don't I!" answers Monica.

Next, without hesitation, the young girl just blurts out, *"I got you, so I get first dibs on snacks next time, that's the deal, remember?"* She crosses her arms, looking all sassy.

"Sure, Kiki, whatever you say," Zack responds.

"ARE YOU TWO DONE? I MEAN, ARE YOU DONE!" Monica said loudly, fed up with her kids' bickering.

Sharon, on the other hand, is quietly grateful that her IUD works just fine as she observes the difficulties this African American woman is having with her biracial children being brats right now. The exquisite joy of not being a mother can be seen clearly in Sharon's eyes.

Sharon turns her attention back to Mr. Lee, choosing to ignore the struggling single mother.

"So, how much do I owe you Mr. Lee?" she asks, ready to check out and leave all the ridiculous noise behind in the store.

"It's on the house." Mr. Lee accommodates his best customer.

"Thank you, Mr. Lee!" Sharon says gratefully, slipping the books he handed her, along with her own, into a shopping bag.

As she's exiting the store, Sharon glances back at the family one more time, feeling grateful that their chaos isn't her responsibility, while the children shoot her a dirty look on her way out.

"You really should teach your children to have good manners, Monica, no offense," Sharon says, being honest.

"And a Motherless woman shouldn't be giving advice to a Parent, no offense, Detective!" Monica fires back with plenty of attitude.

Sharon, annoyed, simply excuses herself because she doesn't have to deal with this nonsense. She has better things to do with her life than engage with a woman wrapped up in chaos.

Once Sharon gets in her vehicle, she heads down to the precinct to check why she received a page from the chief. She takes slow, steady breaths as she drives, letting the rhythm calm her nerves while she's still recovering from Monica's ridiculous rant.

Entering the Police Department, Sharon heads directly to the chief of police to report in.

"So Chief, what's brewing this time in Heightened Hills?" She asks, sounding facetious.

"We have three homicides, and they all look like the same type of killer." As the chief, Charles Dickerson was explaining, Sharon interjects, *"Serial killer,"* displaying her curiosity.

Charles nods in agreement.

"Here are the files. I want you to catch the son of a bitch before he gets to his next victim. Do you understand, Sharon?" The chief said, very direct.

"I'm on it, Chief," Sharon tells him, then excuses herself to get to work.

9

Sharon begins her link analysis and finds that the bodies are located in three different locations of town, forming an odd, thick-looking acute angle shape of some sort. Each body has a Rune carved into it; a Gebo Rune to be exact. They also have two puncture wounds on their necks. As Sharon stares at the two sticks forming an incomplete triangle, she understands why it resembles an acute angle. She knew enough to recognize that the symbol wasn't tied to any real Pagan belief. Whatever this was, it belonged to something twisted and far removed from actual Wiccan practice.

Sharon begins to research the occult and any wicken activities that may have mentioned anything on the dark web or anywhere else, as if they were taking credit for something like human sacrifices. Sharon also notices in the report that the bodies were completely drained of blood.

"What the hell! Am I dealing with wannabe vampires?" she wonders.

Next, Sharon begins sifting through the files, her attention drawn to the one noting that a body had gone missing from the morgue.

The telephone on Sharon's desk rings, cutting through the quiet tension of her office. She straightens, pushing a stack of folders aside before lifting the receiver. *"Richards,"* she answers.

"It's me, Charles. Report to the forensics team; they're down on Hwy. 90. It's one of those damn runes again on a person, but this body is torn to shreds," he informs her.

Sharon feels her stomach tighten. Another body. Another rune. And now torn apart? The pattern that once felt predictable suddenly fractures.

"That's fast. According to the report, the killings took place at least six hours apart from each other. This will make a new record; it's only been two hours," Sharon says, giving her thoughts to the chief. She swivels slightly in her chair, her eyes narrowing as possibilities race through her mind.

Then she continues, *"Torn apart? Don't sound like our guy. This guy has to be someone new or a wannabe copycat, because the guy we're looking for likes to suck blood through the neck, probably using some strange tool."* She concludes, tapping her pen against the desk as the pieces refuse to align.

"Well, you're the Detective, so figure it out. Also, the coroner is down there saying you have to see it just to believe it. They're waiting on you so they can explain their findings a little more in depth, at least that's what they explained to me," Charles tells her.

As Sharon listens, she continues skimming through the case file, her eyes tracking every detail. A line she read earlier suddenly hits her; something the chief mentioned a moment ago now aligns with the report in a way that feels off, almost too convenient.

"Chief, you said Hwy 90?" She asks, wanting confirmation.

"Yes. Why?" Dickerson answers.

"Hwy 90 is where the first body was discovered," Sharon says, her concern sharpening. A chill creeps down her spine. Patterns were supposed to make sense… this one wasn't.

"Sharon, get off this phone, get down there, see what the Hell's going on before this freak gets ahead of us," the chief demands.

"I'm on it," Sharon replies professionally, then hangs up the phone.

The drive out to Hwy. 90 felt heavier than usual, her mind bouncing between possibilities as the scenery blurred past her windows. When she arrived, the forensic team and the coroner were already there, the area taped off under flashing lights. The coroner himself stood off to the side, unusually puzzled, staring at the body bag as if it might start moving on its own.

Sharon ducks under the police tape, boots crunching on gravel as she heads straight to the coroner.

"Okay, what do you got for me, Jeff?" She asks, getting straight to business.

"Well, like I told Charles, you've got to see it to believe it... this is the first cadaver, Mrs. Hart," Jeff explains.

"What do you mean, the first?" Sharon asks, her curiosity spiking.

"Mrs. Hart was literally the first victim, being now rediscovered in the same spot her body was found hours ago," Jeff clarifies, disbelief in his voice. Then he continues, *"And that's not even the strangest part of all this, because check out those fangs... that wasn't there before when I examined her the first time."*

Jeff looks beside himself, eyes wide with confusion and something close to fear.

Sharon looks down at the cadaver, Mrs. Hart, and not only does she notice the two puncture wounds on her neck and the fangs Jeff mentioned, but she also notices how she was ripped into, as if some type of beast had eaten out all the inner body parts from her torso, leaving it bare for all to see. It was licked clean. Mrs. Hart's eyeballs were completely jet black.

Next, Sharon sees the Gebo Rune on Mrs. Hart.

"Why would the murderer want to steal the body from the morgue and bring it back to this very same spot they dropped it off previously, and what the hell did they do to her body?" Detective Richards thinks to herself.

"What's on your mind?" Jeff asks, hoping she can make sense of all of this. However, Sharon is just as puzzled as the coroner; to her, this is starting to turn into a freaky case. An enigma like this is going to take every bit of her focus.

After thinking long and hard, Sharon says to Jeff, *"Okay."* She takes a moment to breathe, then continues, *"We're going to start from the beginning and add on this new information, which means, Jeff, you're gonna have to reexamine the body with this new added information that we're witnessing. I know you don't like it, but if we're gonna get to the bottom of this, we're gonna have to do this by the numbers."* Sharon carefully goes over the plan with Jeff.

"I am not touching that body. There is something ungodly about that thing lying in the dirt, oh hell no, and then

something mauled it to death like it didn't even have a chance. I mean, look at the tracks, you can see Mrs. Hart's footprints and then some type of big beast. They found her and made sure she wasn't gonna stay undead for long, if you get my drift." Jeff was scared out of his wits, his voice trembling as he pointed to the disturbed ground......

"Pull your shit together, Jeff. I need you on this. Come on, man, it's been three hours now. The first three murders were six hours apart, which means if this asshole is gonna strike again, we've got another three hours before he finds his next victim, unless he goes after one of the cadavers we have left. If I get a new coroner, I'll fall behind, so come on, stick with me, Jeff, please!" Sharon makes her case firmly.

"Shit, okay. I'm calling in a friend, no butts." Jeff displays he's dead serious on this one.

"Whatever you need. Let's just hurry because the clock is ticking," Richards responds; her eyes filled with determination that she would bring the killer to justice.

Once the forensic team finishes taking all the photographic evidence they need, they place a body bag down to collect the cadaver. However, the second they start touching Mrs. Hart, the body immediately turns to ash, right in their hands, and the ash itself vaporizes as it hits the ground. Everyone is perplexed, stepping back in shock, their faces tight with disbelief as none of them has ever seen anything like it.

"I guess it's a good thing we got photos, because no one would believe any of this," said Jeff.

Sharon, on the other hand, feels the forensic team and Jeff are just as good, if not better, than the photography when it comes to witnesses. Yet, these are some very strange events, and Sharon has never encountered anything like this in all her years on the force. Not only is her stomach still turning from the grotesque image of what was left of Mrs. Hart's body, but she's still in shock like everyone else over how it just evaporated into nothing.

The detective struggles to piece all of this together, having no prior experience with events like these. Her thoughts feel scattered, slipping between logic and disbelief, and even her training isn't giving her anything solid to hold on to. She's amazed at how this is all playing out, although she wishes someone else were on this case so she could be home enjoying her novels at this point.

With everything happening so fast, her mind starts grasping for direction. Who are we going to call? Who can help? And how? So many questions and yet, no answers in sight.

Sharon and Jeff look at one another, each of them hoping the other has an explanation, but all they can do is stare at each other. Then their eyes shift back to the spot where Mrs. Hart's body had been, now nothing but evaporated ash, leaving them both baffled and silent, unsure what to make of what they just witnessed.

Later, Sharon and Jeff, alongside the team, enter the mortuary. Some of the staff are armed with crosses and wooden stakes, while others carry garlic, clearly rattled by what happened earlier.

15

"Jeff, where's the second victim so we can make sure they're still here and we can make some sense of all this!" Sharon suggests, though she feels the team might be overreacting a bit.

"Mr. Hart's over here, and I'll get his file while Lucy shows you the body," Jeff informs her.

Lucy, a valuable member of the team, not only shows Sharon where the mortuary cabinet is but also pulls open the drawer, revealing a shocking discovery: Mr. Hart has a wooden stake plunged through his heart, and his head was severed from his body, lying beside him.

Without hesitation, Sharon asks Lucy, *"Are there working cameras here? And we also need to check on the third victim immediately to make sure it wasn't tampered with like this one or the other."* Sharon takes charge, urgency tightening in her voice.

"The other body is at a separate funeral home," Lucy says, giving the information.

Sharon then says, *"Call them, hurry,"* her urgency clear.

Lucy immediately takes out her cell phone and places the call.

"You've reached Lively Funeral Homes. If you know the party's extension you are trying to reach, you may enter it now," says the audio answering service. Lucy hesitates for a second, staring at the keypad, then presses the 0, hoping it's the right number. Even though she doesn't actually know the extension, she just needs someone, anyone, to pick up.

"Hello Lucy, what can I do for you?" Jason answers.

"Is the cadaver named Alice Mahu still with you and not vandalized in any way?" Lucy asks, sounding a tad bit upset but still keeping her composure.

"I'll see. Now hold your horses, no reason to rush on this. I'll put you on hold," Jason, the agency working in the funeral home, replies. And before Lucy can utter another word, the line switches to hold.

"I guess we wait," Lucy informs Sharon, tension lingering in her voice.

"At this rate, our chances are just as good as a one-legged man in a sprint race." Sharon's sarcasm slips out, her frustration starting to bubble through the cracks. The team needed a little tension break, and Lucy appreciates Sharon trying to lighten the moment, letting out a soft chuckle despite the pressure weighing on everyone.

After a long minute of waiting that felt like forever, the call finally reconnects. Jason comes back on the line and replies, *"Alice Mahu is still in the mortuary cabinet chilling out,"* his calm, joking tone completely at odds with the panic sitting on Sharon and Lucy's shoulders.

Hearing this, Lucy feels a wave of relief and quickly shares the update with Sharon. Once Detective Richards hears it, the tightness in her chest loosens, if only slightly. At least one thing hasn't gone sideways today.

"So, if that's all, there you go. And why did you ask such an odd question?" Jason asks, now sounding a little weirded out, clearly picking up on the tension he didn't understand.

17

Lucy said, *"You wouldn't believe me if I told you."*

"Try me," Jason replies, sounding cocky.

"Maybe later, but for now, you're a lifesaver, and thank you." She makes a playful kissy noise, *"bye."*

Lucy ends the call in a flirtatious tone, trying to shake off the stress.

"Okay, now what?" she asks, looking to Sharon for answers.

"For now, we wait," Sharon says.

"Wait for what?" Lucy asks, confused.

"At this point, the killer's next move. A lot of this stuff is... It's just unbelievable, and we're gonna need more information. His next move might be the answer we need." Sharon speaks with a confidence she doesn't completely feel, but she needs to sound in control.

"You mean wait for another body to show up?" Lucy asks, disgusted by the thought.

"Got a better plan? I'm listening." Sharon answers, sounding tired and at her wits' end as both women stare at each other, equally frustrated and unsure.

Lucy finally turns and walks away from Sharon, needing air. In her mind, she's convinced this detective might be losing it, and she needs a moment alone before she says something she'll regret.

Jeff walks in with a very handsome man just as Lucy is exiting the area with the mortuary cabinets. Sharon isn't sure how to feel; this man looks like he stepped straight out of a

Heidi Combs romance novel, too perfect for the grim setting they're standing in.

"Sharon, this is Michael Brown, the person I told you I'm calling in to help. Mike, meet Detective Sharon Richards," Jeff says, introducing them. They shake hands in a formal greeting.

"So, Jeff tells me Charles placed you on this case, but what experience do you have hunting down an Upir or a Lycanthrope?" Michael asks, his tone curious and his eyes studying her with genuine interest.

"What is a Upiór, or Lycan?" Sharon beside herself

"Chuckles, I said Lycanthrope, not Lycan. Although sometimes they can be one and the same. A Upiór is another name for a vampire, which, clearly, from what I can see, looks like Mr. Hart was one of your dilemmas. And a Lycanthrope, in short, is someone who can shapeshift from human to animal or wolf," Michael explains with calm confidence.

"Ah, you're an educated man. I like that," Sharon said, genuinely impressed; her eyes lingering on him a moment longer than expected.

"Well, if that pleased you, I have a lot more to teach you," Michael says, his intoxicating, manly voice carrying a confidence that makes Sharon feel unexpectedly attentive. There's something about the way he speaks, calm, assured, almost playful, that pulls her in despite the chaos around them.

19

Sharon simply says, *"Go on,"* her anticipation slipping through before she can stop it.

So, Mike proceeds. *"It's a good thing you have witnesses because vampires don't give off a reflection and therefore, they won't show up in any form of photography. As for the impressions in the mud, that will help your case, along with what type of shape-shifter we could be up against. Now the runes clearly show some type of Wiccan coven is in the mix of all this. A Gebo Rune shows that this coven is trying to do some type of beneficial partnership, and since the victims became vampires, I guess we know who they're trying to be in cahoots with. And before you say it, Detective, no real Pagan or Wiccan coven would ever touch something like this. These kinds of groups twist symbols they barely understand."*

Michael finishes explaining, his eyes fixed on Sharon as if waiting to see whether she truly grasps how deep this situation goes.

"I'm sorry, but do I have to play devil's advocate here? How do you know so much about these things? Hopefully you're not involved," Sharon says, narrowing her eyes as she quietly tests him, weeding out any potential suspects in the room.

Michael doesn't flinch. *"Please, clearly you're in the dark about a great many things, and nothing would be simpler than to keep you in the dark if I were involved in any way,"* he says precariously.

"Or hiding right under my nose might just be the perfect spot," Sharon suggests, her voice low and edged with suspicion.

"I guess being a bit of a ballbuster is okay for a detective," Michael says, settling into the idea that this might just be part of Sharon's personality. He gives her a half-smirk, clearly amused, rather than offended.

Sharon, on the other hand, feels the comment hit differently. *"I'll have you know I actually like a nice pair of balls, thank you very much. I prefer to see it as I'm ruffling your feathers a bit,"* she fires back, giving him sass without hesitation. There's a spark in her tone, equal parts playful and daring.

"Do you two need a room, or what?" Jeff says, raising a brow.

After Jeff makes the remark, Mike gives Sharon a smoldering look, and she surprises herself by enjoying the stare more than she should in the middle of a murder investigation. The brief, almost erotic staring contest ends when Sharon pulls herself together and says, *"Let's get down to business and waste no more time with pleasantries. Mike, I feel if we work together on this, the suspects involved won't be any match for us. Don't you agree?"*

"I agree," Michael replies without hesitation.

"Excellent. We'll go to my place to have the perfect surroundings to concentrate properly," Sharon says, her plan finally coming into focus.

Moments later, at Sharon's place, the two sit together enjoying red wine under slightly dim lights while looking over the files. The room is quiet except for the subtle clink of glass and the soft rustle of papers. Sharon, puzzled, shares her thoughts with Michael. *"What I don't get is, why are*

21

these murders six hours apart? And why isn't there a fourth to keep with the consistency? Why stop at three?"

"I believe with Mrs. Hart's awakening sooner than expected, because most transformations with vampires happen after the funeral, don't ask, I don't know why; however, with that occurring and then the encounter she went through with the Lycanthrope, it caused the killers to take a pause and reflect," Michael offers, his explanation surprisingly compelling.

"Alrighty then, our shape shifters' got everyone spooked. But who are they, and what's with the two lines, the way things were played out in the three separate areas?" Sharon asks, continuing to work through her thoughts. *"I think if we can find the local witch coven, we're closer to some answers,"* she finishes, her mind sharpening on the direction they need to move.

"Hey, this is your town, so who's the locals?" Michael said, adding his logic.

Sharon was listening, but at the same time got lost in Michael's amazing eyes. Unable to hold back any longer, she makes the first move. Sharon let the files slip from her hands and scatter softly across the floor, but she didn't care. In that moment, all she could focus on was the magnetic pull between them. She leaned in, closing the space inch by inch, and pressed her lips to his, slowly at first, as if savoring the gravity of the moment, then with growing certainty as heat stirred in her chest.

As they were making out, she reached down his pants while he was going up her blouse. The heat was so intense; the

22

amazing feeling of his touch set her skin on fire, and the only thing to quench the flames was their lips putting out the blaze.

It's been a while since Sharon has held a well-endowed man. At first, she feels shock in her spine, an awe, followed by confusion as she's using her hand to help her figure out the math equation. Her fingers straining, barely touching, the heat of him burning her palm, a thick pulse throbbing against her skin, her nipples exposed to his tongue now, wet and hot, circling slow, causing her to lose focus but still enjoy his rock hardness; the slick drag of his mouth pulling a gasp from her throat; her back arching. Sharon almost explodes because it's been a while; her breath catching, thighs trembling, a sudden rush of wetness, but manages to hold back.

Between all the intimacy, Sharon hears Michael ask her something she hasn't heard in a long time.

"May I go down on you?" Sked Michael.

The question steals her breath, and Sharon gasps softly, her willingness rising before she can second-guess it. Her pulse jumps, caught between anticipation and the heat of the moment, until her cell phone erupts with the special ringtone she only assigns to urgent calls.

For a split second, she freezes, torn between the urge to say yes to Michael or answer the call. The interruption feels almost cruel. Michael, however, simply reaches for the phone and hands it to her like he's doing her a favor, his expression unreadable.

"Wow, thanks, Mike," Sharon mutters, clearly annoyed as she gently yanks the phone from his hand and answers it.

"Richards," she says, her tone edged with irritation, as if her privacy has been abruptly invaded.

"Detective, we got another body. New location!" Jeff reports, giving her the reason for the call.

"Can it wait?" She pleads, her voice strained from the moment she was dragged out of. But before Jeff can answer, Sharon exhales sharply and cuts him off. *"Just give me the address before I lose my nerve. Don't ask why I have an attitude, just give it to me, Jeff."* Her tone is sharp, firm, and a little too raw.

Jeff gives her the location, and it forces Sharon and Michael to pull themselves out of the moment they were wrapped in. The tension between them lingers in the air for a beat before they both straighten up, gather themselves, and shift their focus back to the case. Within minutes, they're out the door, and moments later, Sharon and Michael are already on the scene.

"Okay, Jeff, what do we have? A bloodsucker or what's left of it?" Michael asks, sounding callous, almost detached. Sharon ignores the tone and begins scanning the area, letting her investigative instincts take over. The night air feels heavier here, like something ugly is still lingering in the shadows.

She notices Lucy nearby, crouched over the new cadaver, taking pictures in silence.

"Has the victim been identified?" Sharon asks Lucy.

"Not yet," Lucy confirms, her camera flashing rhythmically like a heartbeat in the dark.

Not long after, they're all back in the forensics department at the station, reviewing evidence under harsh fluorescent lights. While Sharon studies the spread of photographs, Michael leans in and points to a mark on the victim's shoulder.

"That's a vampire's hieroglyph on her shoulder. I had a friend who ran into a similar case a few years back, it had hieroglyphs in that report too," Michael said, revealing his assessment with a seriousness that wasn't present earlier.

"You said you had what? What happened? And where is this report?" Sharon asks, her voice sharpening as she slips fully into detective mode.

Michael takes a slow breath before answering. *"You would need to get a hold of the Sheriff's Department in Social Falls. It's a town a few miles from here if you want the report. As for my friend... he was up against a pack of Lycanthropes and asked for my assistance because I'm a Shadow Hunter just like him. But that night, I was delayed. Damn it... I should have been there."* His voice cracks slightly, the weight of regret pressing through his words.

Sharon studies him, leaning in just a bit. *"What delayed you, and did he survive?"* she asks, gathering information while gauging the emotional truth behind his expression.

"There was this hot chick who was willing to go down on me that night, and I just didn't want to pass it up. It's not that easy to find someone willing to do those things, you know,"

Michael says, continuing his story with an uncomfortable mix of honesty and regret.

"Yeah, I know exactly what you mean," Sharon replies, her tone relatable but her expression twisting into an odd, sharp look she can't quite hide.

Michael notices immediately, his brow lifting as he reads her reaction. *"Look, that night my buddy died, okay? That's why I handed you the phone. I didn't want you to experience something that could be a déjà vu moment, you know?"* he adds, his voice softening as the regret settles deeper. Then he falls silent, letting the weight of his explanation linger between them.

"Maybe that would have been a déjà vu moment for you, but not me, okay? Yet, I still understand," Sharon replies, her voice steady but edged with a quiet boundary he can't miss.

"Sorry, Sharon. If you give me another chance, I'll make it up to you. What do you say?" Michael asks, trying to mend the tension lingering between them.

"I'll think about it. In the meantime, I need to call Sheriff Krueger of Social Falls to get that report, and anything else that might be useful for this case," Sharon says, shifting her focus back to the investigation.

"You know Sheriff Krueger?" Michael asks, genuinely surprised.

"Uh, yeah," Sharon answers, giving him a look that hints at a deeper story she's not ready to unpack.

A moment later, the call connects.

"So, Sharon, what can I do for you? Because I know this ain't a social call," Krueger answers with a hint of humor threading through his voice.

"Hey, Al, I need some professional courtesy and cooperation on a case that seems quite familiar to one that happened in your town a while back, from what I understand from a Michael Brown, who's with me right now," Sharon said, keeping her tone controlled and businesslike.

"Brown, yeah, I remember him. He and his crazy friend Joseph Green turned my town upside down with their shenanigans… one of my best deputies lost his mind over that whole case. Watch your back, Sharon. There's your professional courtesy and help from me," Sheriff Al Krueger warns, his voice carrying the weight of old frustration.

"Thanks, Al. However, I'm afraid I have a few more questions, and I may need to read your files on the situation, along with talking to your deputy, if he's still around," Sharon replies, leaning forward slightly as she pushes the investigation forward.

"My deputy is at Jennings Institute if you want to speak with him. As for the mass of files on that case, it's yours, just come on down," Krueger says, finishing his part of the conversation.

"Thanks again, Al. I'll be right down," Sharon says, already shifting mentally into the next steps of the investigation.

Moments later, Sharon is driving her standard-issue vehicle with Mr. Brown tagging along in the passenger seat. The tension from earlier lingers faintly in the air, but she keeps her attention on the road. *"You said you and your friend Green were Shadow Hunters. What's that?"* she asks, trying to gather more information as they head toward Social Falls.

"If this is your way of creating small talk while on a ride, you should be a little more subtle about it," Mike replies. Sharon shoots him a quick sideways glance, shrugs, and turns her focus back to the road, still listening.

Michael continues, his voice shifting into something more reflective. *"Joseph... used to hunt strange and unusual things that go bump in the night. And we occasionally worked together to give them a taste of their own medicine. But what happened in Social Falls haunts me to this day. That's... really all I gotta say."* Getting choked up, then goes quiet, staring out the window.

Sharon takes a slow breath. *"Some years ago, my partner and I... I mean, my boyfriend and I, we were on a case to catch a serial killer. To make a long story short, we got a break, checked a lead, and the bastard came way too close to taking us both out. That night still haunts my dreams. Mike... I understand regret. And trying to even the score. So, maybe by us working together, you can get some closure with Joseph. But you've got to be honest with me. No secrets."* She keeps her tone steady, trying to connect with him from a place she rarely opens anymore.

"Sharon, if you don't mind me asking... what was your boyfriend's name?" Michael asks, his voice gentler now, showing solidarity.

"His name was John," Sharon says quietly.

"Hopefully, this case can give us both some much-needed closure. Because we both need it," Michael says, offering his thought with a sincerity she wasn't expecting.

Sharon glances at him for a moment, taking in his words, then turns her eyes back to the road as she thinks about what closure might mean for both of them.

Arriving at the Social Falls Sheriff's Department, Sharon and Michael proceed to meet with the sheriff. They walk up to the counter to speak with the deputy, but before Sharon can even get the words out of her mouth, she hears a familiar voice a few feet behind the counter say, *"Sharon, long time, I see you brought the occult hunter with you,"* Al addressing Sharon.

"Hey Al, sorry this ain't a social visit, pun intended because of the town's name, so can we get on with it if you don't mind, Sheriff." Sharon is straight to business, barely giving him room to respond.

Krueger walks right up to Sharon and Michael, his boots echoing sharply across the floor, then says, *"Well, let's get to it, but first...."*

There's a tension in his stance that Sharon can't quite place. And once Krueger told her that, he cold-cocked Michael right in the chin without warning, knocking him straight out. The sound of the hit cracks through the room like a gunshot.

"That's for Henry, bitch!" Krueger said, talking directly to an unconscious Michael, his anger raw and unfiltered.

"I can see you gentlemen have something to work out. May I speak with your deputy first, who was on this case, and then

I can go over the files while you and Mike catch up on old times?" Sharon suggests, stepping lightly out of the tension unfolding in front of her.

"Sure, why not. I told you where he is… just ask for Henry Snowden," Krueger informs her, still glaring down at the unconscious Michael like the punch didn't fully satisfy him.

So, Sharon goes to Robert Jennings Mental Asylum Institute. Once inside, she approaches the front desk and says, *"Henry Snowden,"* as she presents her badge.

"Detective, I'm afraid, unless you have some type of court order of some kind, you're gonna have to talk to the head doctor. Don't worry, she's here." The orderly at the desk informs her with a sadistic smile, the kind that makes Sharon instantly uneasy.

Moments later, Sharon is inside Doctor Hemingway's office.

"Please, Detective, have a seat. I am Doctor Hemingway, and I am the head director of this institute. How may I help you?" Hemingway says; her pleasant demeanor almost too controlled.

"I need to speak with Deputy Henry Snowden. I'm working on an official case, and he has some information that could be vital to my investigation. That's all I can share with you, I hope you can understand, Doctor," Sharon replies, being forthcoming but firm.

"I understand, Detective. However, Henry is a special case; he is under my direct care, and therefore, if you say or ask anything that can cause his fragile psyche to crack, I am liable. So, I am afraid I need a little more detail than that.

Please. " The doctor's tone is polite but very direct, leaving no room for misunderstanding.

"Well, Doctor, I'll make it clear for you, by you not letting me speak with him, you are interfering in an official investigation, and therefore I could have you run in. So why don't we just pass all this ridiculousness and let me talk to the deputy!" Sharon says, her voice tightening as she applies pressure.

"No need for threats, detective. Keep in mind, I do house the criminally insane here, so why don't you just have some professional courtesy? I'm sure you can understand, right!" Hemingway says, trying to bring down the temperature.

Then she continues, *"If I let you speak with him, may I record the session? It's purely for research, of course, as well as any possible chance of helping Henry in his recovery. Surely you can understand because of the unique circumstances surrounding Henry, of course."* Hemingway does her best to reason with the detective.

"I agree. Now, may I talk to Henry?" Sharon asks, trying to stay calm.

"But of course, detective," Hemingway answers, sounding elusive in a way that immediately keeps Sharon on edge.

Chapter 2

As Sharon enters the padded room, she sees Henry sitting in a corner, confined in a straitjacket, not even looking like a shadow of his former self. Instead, he looks like a lost cause; empty, distant, and completely disconnected from the world around him. The cold, cushioned walls swallow the little sound in the room, making each step Sharon takes feel heavier.

Sitting at the suggested safe distance, Sharon attempts to communicate with Henry.

"Deputy Snowden, I'm Detective Sharon Richards. I have a few questions to ask you. Do you think you can do that for me, deputy, please, officer to officer?" Sharon asks, hoping to reach his better angels.

"Are you Alpha? I can hear the Howl calling out to me. Release me. Free me from this pain, Alpha. It hurts; it burns." Henry pleads to Sharon while using body gestures to reference the jacket and how it needs to come off. His movements are frantic and desperate, tugging at the restraints like they're burning him from the inside.

Sharon notices his jacket has some type of medium to dark blue-purple color to it, nothing like the typical white or beige straightjacket she's used to seeing. The odd coloration sends a small ripple of concern through her.

"Deputy Snowden, I told you I'm a Detective," Sharon says, attempting to reiterate what she just said before, feeling he's a bit confused or trapped in some delusion.

However, Henry interjects, his voice booming from deep inside a fractured mind.

"If you are not Alpha, be gone from me, for you are no better than the enemy who has me bound!"

Henry's extreme rage pours out so violently that it echoes off the padded walls. Sharon feels whoever Henry Snowden once was is now gone, at least not in the person sitting in front of her, because that man is just nuts. As the reality sank in, her mind began connecting the dots and understanding why Krueger had knocked Mike out earlier; whatever had happened to Henry had changed him into something unstable and unpredictable. She goes to the door and requests to leave the padded room.

As she was leaving the room, Sharon couldn't help noticing the rough bruising on his wrists, the kind that comes from when people are held in police cuffs for way too long. She swallowed the question rising in her throat. This wasn't the time to start pointing fingers, but something here wasn't sitting right, nor was someone being treated right.

"Thank you for letting me talk with him. I see now my answers are only in the files now, before he went mad," Sharon says, coming to this conclusion as she shares her thoughts with the doctor.

"It's fine, Detective. Still, thank you for speaking with him because it does help to understand where his state of mind is, and for that, thank you." Doctor Hemingway's voice is calm, almost sounding insidious beneath the politeness.

However, Sharon thinks nothing of it and says, *"You're welcome, Doc."*

Once back at the Sheriff's Station, Sharon asked Krueger, *"How's Mike? Did you fellas work out your issues? I hope you both did!"* having a bit of optimism in her voice.

"He's still talking crazy. I should have locked him up instead of ignoring him last time. Just go with Alex, he'll take you to the jail department where you can speak with him," Krueger told her that he had thrown Mike in a holding cell.

For a moment, Sharon wondered what could've happened between the two of them to make Krueger actually lock Michael up, but she pushed the thought aside; she had a case to work on, and that came first. *"The files. I wanna see them first, then I'll go speak with him, he's not going anywhere,"* said Sharon, eager to get to the bottom of this.

So, Krueger gives her the files, and Sharon begins looking for anything helpful. It was already dark by the time Sharon and Michael got to Social Falls, and now it's lingering into the late night. Sharon is tired, but still determined to get to the bottom of this. As she reads, she begins to notice things like patterns, a unicursal hexagram designed to mark the locations of each victim. An ending where it began at George Hemingway's hospital in the town.

Sharon writes down the name *"Hemingway"* in her notes. *"What does this mean?"* She ponders to herself.

As she looks over more papers, it appears that Deputy Snowden was acting in the capacity of a detective, investigating these murders, piecing things together, and three suspects stood out. The Hemingway Foundation, Joseph Green, and a Michael Brown. As Sharon read Michael's name in the report, she gasped. Fear gripped her as she struggled to remain optimistic, hoping he was just a lead and not something more dangerous. She read on, desperate for any hope in sight.

Finally, by the end of the report, she sees that Michael wasn't there at the hospital. The report ends with Joseph Greene's body being recovered. Apparently, it fell from a high position, falling out of a window of the hospital. Although, according to the coroner, Joseph apparently was already dead from his body being horribly mauled by some animal before falling out of the window and hitting the ground. But how? There is no animal of any kind in the report, and the hospital security cameras were down that night.

Page after page felt like someone had taken a pair of scissors to the truth. Notes missing, timestamps off by minutes that mattered, statements that sounded coached. It wasn't sloppy work; it looked like sabotage. Sharon clenched her jaw. She'd seen reports doctored before, but never this blatantly. What the hell were they trying to bury?

However, one thing the reports clearly noted was that the group wasn't a traditional Pagan circle, but a fringe occult sect that had broken away from anything resembling real spiritual practice.

When morning broke, Sharon went to talk with Michael.

"What were you and Joseph doing here? What were you allegedly hunting?" Sharon, feeling entitled to know.

"We were hunting a vampire coven only to run into an eclectic coven that was being overrun by a pack of lycanthropes. On our last night here, if I hadn't been delayed, I could have been there for Joseph. I wish I were," Michael admits.

"Based on the information you told me, you weren't delayed; it's more like you were distracted... men," Sharon says, disgusted by his lame explanation, the disappointment showing clearly in her voice.

"Oh, yeah? What's the bloody reason that got you distracted that you couldn't be there for your boyfriend? Or why you left me here to rot in this jail cell last night, huh?" Michael snaps back, upset and losing his temper.

"Stay focused. This ain't about me, this is about you. Now, answer my questions, or you'll stay in that cell." Sharon is very stern in her statement, her glare sharp enough to cut through his defensiveness.

Michael understands immediately that he has to go along with this or he'll be rotting here indefinitely, just by the way Sharon is glaring at him. *"Fuck!"* Michael replies, frustration boiling over before he forces himself to breathe and calm down. Then, softening his tone, he says, *"Okay, okay... What do you want to know?"* Michael, expressing cooperation at last.

So, Sharon begins, *"Who is this alleged Vampire Coven, and why didn't you guys cooperate better with Henry?"* Giving her best bad cop routine, leaning into the pressure she knows he responds to.

"Deputy Snowden was marked with a Vampire Hieroglyph, so yeah, can't trust him," Michael says, sarcastically but telling the truth. Afterwards, he goes on, *"Besides, by the time the shape shifters came into focus, I was D... distracted, there I said it."* Michael coming clean; his frustration slipping through.

"Sacred writing, hocus pocus crap, just cut the shit and level with me, OK? I ain't got time for these ridiculous occult games that you believe in. An officer of the law lost their mind behind all this stupid stuff, and I'm not about to lose mine, but I promise you, you'll go first before I do. Now, tell the truth, why didn't you work with the deputy, or are you a part of the crap that's going on? Talk." Sharon, laying it on thick, the intensity in her tone cutting like a blade.

"I'll make it plain for you, Detective. You think you've seen some things on the streets, you believe you've been in the SHIT, the world you think exists is just cookies and cream and all that nice stuff, that's the crap. You and Krueger, with your Qualified Immunity B.S., acting with impunity. Because without witnesses or video, I don't even have a shot in court to prove excessive force was even used, or that you were an accomplice in the crime. So, let's be honest. You see, beneath this mirage of snake oil that you call society, there's a world beneath it, the real world. It's not a subculture, where knowledge truly is power, but if you don't wield it, it's wasted on you." Michael scolds Sharon with a raw, unfiltered edge.

Sharon isn't sure how to respond because there seems to be some truth in his statements. Nevertheless, she tries to press on, *"Look, no one wants to hear that bullshit. Your utter contempt for society, if you don't like this one, get out and find one that you do. But in the meantime, I'm gonna ask you one more time why you and Joseph were there. The truth this time."* Sharon, cracking down on Mike, refusing to be thrown off.

"You don't want to believe me, fine, but I will not make up a story just to suit your unwillingness to look beyond the veil," Mike told Sharon, his voice worn thin with irritation and exhaustion. Then he lay down on the jail bed and rested his eyes, turning his back to her as if he had finally given up trying to convince her of anything.

"The Veil? What the hell are you talking about?" Sharon Confused

"Look, I'm not going anywhere. So, when you finally see the world I'm talking about, come bail me out, then we'll talk," Michael says, his tone flat but certain, like he already knows she won't believe him until reality forces her hand.

Sharon pondering on his words, then said, *"And what if I never see this world you speak of?"* making more of a rhetorical statement than a question.

"Form what I saw, and from what Jeff told me, the things happening in Heightened Hills are similar to how things went down in this very town... I'll see you soon," Michael said calmly, almost with an eerie certainty that unsettled her.

Sharon holds a good poker face, but deep down inside, there was something in the tone of his voice and his demeanor that made her feel he was telling the truth. She doesn't want to admit it, not even to herself. *"How do you know Jeff?"* Sharon tries to keep him talking, fishing for any useful detail,

38

but Michael just remains silent, shutting down the conversation entirely.

"Okay, suit yourself. Why don't you give me a call when you're tired of thawing out here?" Sharon says, giving an attitude as she leaves the jail area. Now entering Krueger's office, Sharon asks, *"What's the big deal with you and Mike, huh?"* trying to get a sense of things from another angle.

"That guy knows things. Henry was actually on to something, but that guy and his friend who died mysteriously withheld certain information that could have helped my deputy from going insane and even probably cracking this case. Hell, even as I look over some of this stuff, it doesn't make a lot of sense; there are a lot of gaps and other stuff. But I know he's the key since he's the remaining living witness to what this puzzle could mean." The sheriff, looking like a man at the cusp of solving a conspiracy, the weight of the unsolved pieces pressing hard on him.

However, Sharon noticed that there was a kind of anger in the way Krueger was telling her about Mike and Henry; not fear, she didn't fear any man, but recognition. She'd seen that look before on cops who took things too far and dared anyone to call them out on it. Though she brushed the thought aside, but it didn't go quietly.

"Hey, Al, why don't you get some sleep? You look like you could use some." Sharon taking notice and trying to comfort him. *"Practice what you preach,"* Krueger getting snippy.

"Okay, let's both take a break and get some sleep, and we'll meet back up later, an hour or two maybe," Sharon suggests.

Krueger nods in agreement, so Sharon excuses herself and goes to check into the local motel.

While there, trying to get some rest on a roughly comfortable bed, she finds it impossible to relax. Her body keeps reminding her of everything left unfinished. A slow, throbbing tension that rolls through her with every breath she takes, followed by a deep aching discomfort running wild through her, and a heavy feeling that is being multiplied by muscle contractions along her clitoris, labia, and pelvis.

Sharon now begins to realize that because she did not climax earlier due to her and Mike being interrupted, she's experiencing Blue Vulva Syndrome.

"Just great, I hate when this happens," she mutters, hopelessly frustrated, irritated by the pressure building with no release. She has no vibrator, and she's sick of masturbating alone. The tension pulses through her body, making sleep nearly impossible.

Chapter 3

Zack and Kiki are home alone while their mom is taking care of some important business. Zack, twelve, notices his little sister Kiki, ten, wearing her hooded poncho and staring out their living room window at the neighbor across the way. With her arms crossed, Kiki studies Miss Hon's yard, where the woman has planted lots of Aconitum around her house.

"What's with that old lady always giving us dirty looks? I don't like her or her choice in gardening," Kiki voices her opinion, sounding both annoyed and suspicious.

"I hear in Chinese culture, they use those types of plants as herb medicine for pain. That's at least what Mom said," Zack replies, trying to sound informed while keeping an eye on his sister's intense stare.

"Whatever," Kiki said, just shrugging it off as unimportant. Then, as she glares at Miss Hon, Kiki begins to hum a beautiful yet mysterious and bone-chilling melody, the kind that doesn't seem to belong in a child's throat.

"Mom gave us strict instructions to stay inside and to go nowhere... Ohh, I like Miss Hon's Jack-o'-Lantern on her porch. Very creative," Zack says, reminding his antsy sister of their mom's rules but getting easily distracted by the glowing pumpkin outside.

"You're no fun," Kiki expresses her boredom, rolling her eyes.

"Look, Halloween is tomorrow, okay? We'll scare and get all the sweets and candy we want. Besides, it's supposed to

be a full moon tomorrow night, that might be fun, " Zack tells her.

"Like a full moon really matters, come on now. Anyway, just remember our deal, I get first dibs on the snacks, OK? And I bet Miss Hon..." Kiki replies, but suddenly stops because they hear an eerie noise coming from somewhere outside.

The sound cuts through the quiet of the house. The children freeze, looking toward the yard. They don't know exactly where it came from, only that it was close. Startled, but still trying to be brave, they glance at each other.

"Do you think it's...?" Zack starts to ask Kiki, but again an *odd noise cuts him off. This time it comes from the rooftop, a slow, deliberate thump like someone heavy is pacing above them. Both children go still.*

As Zack and Kiki anxiously listen to the noise, everything goes eerily quiet, the kind of silence that makes the hair on the back of their necks stand up. On the roof, however, the vampire can smell the fear of the children. It crawls closer, hesitating only when it catches another scent; something far more dangerous, something that sends fright straight into its undead heart.

Before it can escape, a deep growling noise emerges right beside it on the roof. The vampire turns, but too late, its head is bitten clean off by the werewolf. With every bite, the sound of bones crunching fills the night as the werewolf chews through what's left.

Miss Hon saw what happened on the roof, and she was terrified to her wits' end. Her elderly frame trembled, but

42

before she could even process the horror, her grandson cried out, *"Grandma, hurry, get inside!"* The young man had witnessed it too, panic sharpening his voice. As she hastened back into the house, the beast on the roof was still busy enjoying its meal, chewing with a wet, nauseating rhythm. She managed to close the door; however, after some time, the sound vanished into sudden silence as the latch clicked.

Moments later, Monica returned home to find the children playing.

"So, was everything fine while I was gone?" she asked.

"Well, Mom, that depends on how you define fine," Zack said, being cheeky.

Monica smiled at his humor. *"Other than some odd noises, everything was fine,"* Kiki replied.

Monica, now looking suspicious and hiding something behind her back, suddenly revealed the video game the kids had been wanting. She presented it to them, and Zack lit up. *"Oh, thanks, Mom, you're the best!"*

Kiki followed with her own excitement: *"Yeah, thanks, Mom!"*

Later that night, as Monica was playing video games with the kids, Kiki asked, "Mom, why is tomorrow so special, and not just for us but for others?" Her eyes were full of curiosity, and Zack wore the same look.

"Well, my pumpkin cub darlings, it's like this…" Monica began to explain, but a sudden knock on the door cut her off. When she answered it, a police officer stood there and asked,

43

"Sorry to disturb you this night, ma'am; however, are you Monica Strode?" He waited for her response.

"Strode is my maiden name; it's Summers now," Monica replied.

"Okay, do you have a sister by the name Lisa Strode?" the officer asked.

"Why yes... oh God, did something happen? Is she OK?" Monica asked, worry tightening her voice.

"Ma'am, I feel it'd be best if you just come with us down to the station and we can discuss this more privately," the officer suggested, with two others standing behind him.

"Mom, is everything okay? Did something happen to Auntie Lisa?" Zack asked, confusion and fear blending across his expression.

"I don't know. You and your sister get your jackets, let's go," Monica answered. While Zack did as told, Kiki just stood there, teary-eyed and terrified. Monica grabbed her daughter's jacket, draped it around her shoulders, and hurried the children out the door with the police.

Later at the station, an officer said, *"Ma'am, I'm Detective Sparrow, and I am truly sorry to have to inform you that your sister was shot and killed earlier tonight. She has already been properly identified."*

Before the detective could finish, Monica broke down, sobbing bitterly. *"Lisa!"* she cried, mourning her sibling. Deep down, she was grateful the police had the children in the next room, occupied with video games while she faced this devastating news. She wasn't looking forward to telling them, but first she had to steady herself. Moments like this demanded everything in her; she had to dig deep and stay strong for them. They were exposed without her, vulnerable in a world that took more than it ever gave. She needed to be their foundation.

"Once again, I'm truly sorry for your loss, Mrs. Summers. However, I must ask you, do you know anyone who might want to harm your sister or your family in general, possibly someone who dislikes you and might retaliate by targeting your loved ones?" the detective asked.

"Retaliate… are you trying to imply something, detective?" Monica said, instantly on the defensive.

"I'm sorry, but I need to cover all my bases here and make sure nothing is overlooked," the officer told her.

Monica responded, *"Am I under arrest or being detained, officer?"* wanting a clear answer.

"No," he said.

Monica immediately excused herself, retrieved her kids from the next office, and stormed out of the station, her frustration simmering beneath the grief.

Chapter 4

Sharon is awakened by her cell phone going off.

"Where have you been? I've been trying to reach you all this time, what the hell?" Jeff says, sounding angry.

"I've been trying to sleep off some frustration, sorry," Sharon replies.

"Frustration of what exactly, this case?" Jeff presses.

Not wanting to give out any TMI, Sharon gets straight to business. *"Just tell me what you've got, Jeff. Did you find anything? What?"*

"I did an analysis of all the blood we collected at the recent victim location, and I checked each sample with the national DNA database," Jeff informs her.

Sharon cuts in, *"I thought only the FBI had access to that database."*

"I know a guy who knows a guy," Jeff says, sounding more questionable than he likely intends. *"Anyway, only one blood sample matched the database, and that's a Catherine Winslow. She's right here in town."*

"Awesome. What time is it?" Sharon asks.

"Ten in the morning. Why?" Jeff answers.

"Holy shit, I slept a whole day away," Sharon said, surprised.

"Yeah, happy Halloween. Now, are you done up there in Social Falls so you can get back down here in Heightened Hills and we can solve this case?" Jeff asked, eager to know.

"Not quite yet, but I'm close. Just categorize everything the way I like it, Jeff. Once I'm done here, I'll let you know when I'm coming, and we'll hit the ground running, OK?" Sharon told him.

"Sure, whatever you say, Detective," he replied, sounding a bit annoyed.

Sharon picked up on it and softened her tone. *"Jeff, thanks. I really appreciate you. I want you to know that,"* she said sincerely.

"No problem," Jeff replied.

Sharon continued, *"Jeff, how do you know Michael? I mean... how did y'all meet?"*

"Mike and I go way back. Other than being one of my colleagues, he and I helped each other with certain leads in important cases like the one we're on. I act as his guy when it comes to peculiar law enforcement cases tied to the occult. And when I need information about the underworld of the occult, he becomes my informant. I see it as mutual cooperation in critical cases," Jeff told her.

"Look, as a cop, I completely understand the importance of reliable guides and leads, especially in the weird cases like this one. I get it, and I respect it. I just hope you're using caution when sharing information with Mike and keeping fellow cops safe," Sharon said.

"Of course. What type of man or cop do you think I am, Sharon?" Jeff sounded offended.

"I'm just giving some friendly advice, that's all, Jeff," she said, defending her point.

"Sounds more like distrust to me," he muttered before ending the call.

Sharon, realizing she may have messed up, however, can't focus on that right now and tries to reach out to Sheriff Krueger. She places the call, but it just rings for a while, then goes to voicemail. It's fifteen after ten, so she throws the covers off and rushes to take a shower and get ready.

At the station, Sharon asked, *"Where's the Sheriff?"*

"He hasn't checked in since he clocked out late last night," the deputy behind the counter expounds.

Sharon goes to Krueger's home and knocks. After getting no response from knocking or ringing the doorbell, she grabs the hideaway key. Once in, and receiving no response after calling out to him, she pulls her sidearm as a precaution and begins to search for him. Looking around, she notices papers and other types of things posted up on the walls and boards as if Krueger was really deep into some conspiracy theory he was desperately trying to crack in his town. Sharon goes deeper into the house, stepping over and around papers and boxes.

Sharon slowly enters the sheriff's bedroom, and to her surprise, she sees a beautiful young woman dressed in a black cloak outfit, using some type of magical spell, sucking the life essence out of Krueger as he's lying helplessly in bed.

"Freeze, bitch!" Exclaims Sharon.

However, the mysterious person, feeling unopposed, quickly waves her hand, lifting Sharon up and pinning her against the wall in the bedroom while she continues to finish the job on the sheriff. Sharon, by now pissing in pants and thinking, *"Ohh God, I'm next,"* has tears streaming down her cheeks as she is gripped in fear.

Krueger, lying down as a lifeless, dried-up raisin in the bed, draws the young lady's gaze before she turns her eyes toward Sharon. Sharon screams in horror, *"No, help!"* Her heart pounding out of her chest. In shock and about to pass out, she suddenly crashes to the floor. Shaking, she looks up only to see Krueger's rotting corpse in the bed while she's on the floor, the mysterious young lady now gone. Sharon realizes she lost her cool there, yet she's so grateful to still be alive; cries tears of raw relief.

"Is this the world Mike was talking about? If so, I need to bail him out pronto. How am I still here, or am I a spirit?" Sharon thinks to herself, dozens of thoughts going round and round in her mind. She checks her own pulse, paying attention to her breathing and eventually convinces herself she is still alive, then lifts herself off the floor. Sharon next picks up her weapon, which she dropped when she was tossed against the wall, and holsters it.

Detective Sharon Richards, rattled to her core, isn't even sure how to feel. *"What the hell?"* she whispers, still in shell shock. The scene replays in her mind, the swirling wind, the impossible pull of dark magic, the way that mysterious woman drained the sheriff's life essence as if stealing his

49

soul. It was horrifying, unreal, something no training could have prepared her for.

But the worst part is the question she can't shake: Why was she spared?

Why did the creature look at her and choose to let her live?

Sharon stands there trembling, drowning in questions with not a single answer in sight. *Next Sharon faints.*

"Sharon, can you hear me?" Charles asked her.

Sharon was at Hemingway Hospital being treated for trauma while her boss came down to check on her.

"What happened? How did I get here?" Sharon wanting answers

"The neighbor heard your screams and called 911. By the time deputies were on the scene, you were comatose," Chief Dickerson explained.

Next, he asked, *"Sharon, what happened? Can you recall?"*

"You wouldn't believe me even if I told you. I don't even know if I wanna believe it myself," Sharon said, still in disbelief.

Chapter 5

Moments later, Sharon waited to be released from the hospital, the events at Krueger's home still replaying behind her eyes like a nightmare she couldn't wake from. The more she tried to piece it together, the more one truth kept surfacing: she needed Mike. Whatever she saw in that house wasn't something she could face alone. Without his insight into the supernatural, she'd be lost in the dark.

It was a hard truth, but she forced herself to accept it. Hopefully, if anything good could come from this mess, it would be solving the case… and maybe finishing what she and Mike had started back at her home before everything spiraled. Business before pleasure, she reminded herself, even though the two were starting to blur in dangerous ways.

Getting Mike out of jail, Sharon fills him in on what's been happening.

"Looks like you've been busy," Mike replied.

"No shit, so looking at the files and what I told you, where should we go from here?" Sharon asked, hoping for answers.

"We go back to Heightened Hills, because Catherine… I mean, Cathy is our key," Michael tells her.

"Why do you call her Cathy? Do you know her?" Sharon asks, wanting to understand.

"She's the one who gave me the BJ," Michael explains, but Sharon cuts him off and says, *"I get it, I don't like her already.*

Let's talk to the bitch, more like me, not you, though." Sharon makes clear.

Coming to Cathy's place, Sharon knocks on the door.

"Open up, police!" She demands.

A beautiful young lady with an undercut answers the door.

"When did shadow hunters start working with cops?" Cathy asks, being sassy.

"I ask the questions here, not you," Sharon tells her, then makes her assume the position and frisks her down for weapons.

After the pat-down, she goes on to say, *"Now, where were you during the hours of 3 a.m. and 4 yesterday, huh?"* Sharon is not playing around.

"What is this about, copper? I'm not saying anything without my lawyer," Cathy says, standing her ground.

"We got your DNA at the crime scene, bitch!" Sharon says, wanting her to understand. Next, Sharon took out her cuffs and made the arrest.

Chapter 6

Down at the office, Sharon questions Cathy with Michael by her side.

"So why were you there? Tell us what you know!" Said Sharon.

"I want my phone call, copper," Cathy insists.

"Cathy, please, talk to us. Lives are on the line here!" Michael pleads, his voice steady but urgent.

"Okay, but only to you, not her," Cathy says, being honest.

"You're not sucking his dick again, bitch!" Sharon protests, the jealousy sharp and unfiltered.

"Is that what this is about?" Cathy asks, beside herself.

"No," Michael says, then continues, *"Just tell us what you know."*

"Look, some people in black hoodies took me and some girl to this place, cute marks in our arms, put us on our knees for what seemed to me demons in flesh," Cathy tells them, her voice trembling now. *"After the demon was done with the woman, I was next. If it wasn't for that werewolf showing up, I'd be dead."* She shows the mark once she stops speaking. It was a Gebo Rune.

"I haven't left my place since," Cathy says, scared.

Michael: *"The people in black, were they males and females?"*

53

Cathy: *"Yes."*

Michael: *"These demons in flesh, did they have jet black eyeballs?"*

Cathy: *"Yes!"* Her eyes flick around the room, like she expects one to appear.

Michael*: "Those men and women are witches and warlocks, a coven, while the demons are vampires."*

Cathy sits in silence, absorbing the truth as if it's too heavy to hold. Mike turns to Sharon and says, *"Let's talk in the hallway."* After they step out of the room, Michael tells her quietly, *"Your coven is looking for Catherine. Alice Mahu will be a vampire soon enough. And clearly this coven is making a pact with vampires for land, and the werewolf is not having it."*

"What are you saying, Michael? What does all this mean?" Sharon asks, wanting clarity she's not sure she wants.

"We're in the middle of a turf war," Michael says.

Chapter 7

Michael and Sharon go over to check on Alicia Mahu. As they enter the mortuary, Lucy meets them and says with a smile, *"Mahu is still chilling out for now."*

"Awesome, now let's wait for her to wake up," Michael explains.

Sharon: *"Huh..."* Not quite understanding.

"The cadaver is becoming a vampire now, remember," Michael reminds her.

"Oooh, yeah," Sharon says, the clarity hitting her.

As they come to the body bag on the table it's open from the zipper, and empty. The inside of the bag is cold and slightly damp, but Alicia Mahu is nowhere in sight. Terrified, they look around to see if they can find her anywhere, the room feeling suddenly too still, too quiet, as if something is holding its breath with them.

Lucy looks up, drawn by the faintest shift in the air, only to see Alice giving her a vicious-looking smile, jet black eyeballs and vampire fangs gleaming in the dim light. The smile isn't human; it stretches too wide, too slow, like something wearing a person's skin and learning how to mimic joy. Lucy stands there, horror-struck, her knees weakening as a cold wave rolls across the room, the air heavy with the sour smell of decay.

Alice's head tilts in a sharp, unnatural twitch, bones cracking faintly under the motion. Then her muscles coil, her body arching like a creature ready to pounce. She lunges, limbs snapping forward with sickening speed, her nails scraping the air like she's already imagining them buried in Lucy's throat.

But before she can reach her, Michael steps in front of Lucy, thrusting a cross out with both hands.

"Down, bitch! Go back!!" Michael commands. Alice is repelled by the object, screaming in pain.

The trio runs for an exit, but they're cut off by the vampire. Lucy bolts toward the receiving dock, and Sharon and Michael follow. Once upstairs by the doors, Alice closes in with a sinister crawl. Lucy throws open the dock doors, letting sunlight flood in. Alice disintegrates and dissolves into nothing. Feeling safe now, Michael, Sharon, and Lucy head back to the precinct.

Coming to Cathy's questioning room, Sharon says, *"You're in witness protection now, you okay with that?"* Making sure they're on the same page.

"Oh, hell yeah!" Cathy replies.

After clearing everything with the Chief, Sharon and Cathy, with Michael, get to a safe house. Once there, Michael tells Sharon, *"I'm going to go get some supplies. I'll be back,"* then leaves. It's now just Sharon and Cathy inside.

Ten minutes later, Cathy asks, *"So what's next? When do I get a new ID and such?"* Curious.

Sharon thinks, then responds, *"For now, we sit tight,"* hoping that was a good answer.

Suddenly, the wooden front door shatters, and emerging into the doorway is the beautiful black-cloaked woman from before, holding up Commissioner Dickerson's severed head.

"Run…!!!" Sharon shouts to Cathy. Sharon sends bullets downrange, only for the cloaked figure to slow them mid-air and toss them aside. Sharon runs harder while Cathy is already gone.

Sharon struggles to stay vigilant as she calls out for Cathy, but Cathy is nowhere to be found. Then she hears a sarcastic cackle of women. Looking out the window, she sees witches flying away using part of their cloaks as wings. They're carrying Cathy, bound and gagged.

"Bitches, man," Sharon mutters, furious. Next, she realizes it's all tied to the turf war.

As she comes out of the house, Sharon runs into Michael.

"Where is Cathy?" Michael asks.

"Those bitches got her," Sharon tells him in a frustrated way.

Chapter 8

A small choir sings a haunting tune in a cappella as the witches carry Cathy inside the last victim's location. Their voices echo unnaturally, vibrating off the walls like the hum of something ancient waking up. The sound is hollow and cold, brushing against Cathy's skin like icy fingertips. The air grows thick with the scent of damp earth, burning herbs, and something metallic, blood, old and dried.

The hooded woman from the safe house stands in front of her and says, *"Now on your knees, Sacrifice,"* ordering Cathy down. The coven forces her to the floor, their hands cold and rigid, almost claw-like. Witches and warlocks stand in a tight circle, presenting her as an offering to the vampires lurking in the swallowing darkness.

Cathy screams as the vampires approach her, their footsteps silent yet somehow heavy, as if the floor sinks beneath them. Their jet-black eyes shine like wet stones, and their fangs glint with fresh hunger. The air around them seems to collapse inward, carrying a sour, corpse-like odor

Then, suddenly, they halt mid-lunge. Every vampire freezes in place, limbs rigid, faces twisted, as a wolf's howl echoes through the building. The sound is not just heard but felt; it vibrates through Cathy's bones, slicing through the chamber like a blade of sound. The temperature drops sharply, breath frosting in the air.

A Lycanthrope bursts into the room.

The thing is massive, fur rippling like liquid shadow, eyes burning with feral gold. It tears into the vampires instantly, ripping them apart like shredded turkey. Bones crack. Flesh hits the floor. Blackish blood splatters across the walls as the coven scatters in terror, their robes whipping around them as the choir's chanting collapses into panicked shrieks.

After the werewolf makes short work of the enemy, he turns to Cathy. His breath hits her skin, hot, wild, animal, and the musk of predator and blood fills her lungs. He lowers his head and bites her shoulder, sharp pain exploding through her nerves.

Then he turns away, leaving her on the cold floor.

Cathy catches a blurred glimpse of the werewolf's massive balls swinging as he moves, the image burned into her fading sight before her vision collapses and she passes out.

Chapter 9

As Sharon was looking through the files from Henry, she saw each location of the victims perfectly aligned to create a unicursal hexagram. Her stomach tightened as the realization hit, and she gripped the folder harder while they raced to save Cathy, with Mike driving.

"What happened in Social Falls is now happening in Heightened Hills. This turf battle… It's getting crazy by the minute," Sharon said, sharing her epiphany with Mike. Her voice trembled with urgency.

Next, she called for backup to meet her at the location they were headed to, but dispatch responded with, *"Sorry, Detective, we've got to respond immediately to a call for help from the sheriff's department out in Social Falls. It appears to be some type of terrorist attack happening at the Jennings Asylum."* He explained in haste, and then the call suddenly cut out.

"Hello? HELLO!" Sharon shouted, but there was no response. She tried to get a hold of Jeff next, but got nothing.

"OK, Michael, I didn't get a chance to ask you, but now, tell me… how does Cathy know that you are a shadow hunter, and what the hell is going on?" Sharon asked, confused and scared, her pulse hammering as the road ahead blurred by.

Michael lets out a slow breath before answering Sharon's question, eyes fixed on the road as if choosing the right words might keep everything from collapsing further.

"In short, Cathy was my apprentice, but I walked away from her after Joseph died. I kind of blamed her for that whole thing. The turf war… It's real, like I told you. What Jennings Institute is going through is not a terrorist attack, at least not in the way you think. That asylum is controlled by the vampires' network along with Hemingway Hospital. When dispatch said they were under attack, I have a pretty good idea who it is," Michael says, his tone low and tense.

"Who?" asked Sharon.

"The wolf pack. And their numbers are growing. I cut down a few werewolves on my way back to you," Michael reveals, the weight of it heavy in the small space of the car.

"Damn it, Mike, you should have told me this stuff sooner. I said no secrets," Sharon snaps, very upset with him.

"Well, you should have never left me in jail," Mike points out.

"Not now, Mike!" Sharon yells back, frustration and fear colliding in her voice as the situation spirals.

After what felt like a lovers' quarrel, they arrived on the scene. Michael immediately began placing Jack-o'-lanterns made from turnips in four directions surrounding the place, each one filled with burning sage. Smoke drifted low along the ground, giving the air a strange, ritualistic heaviness.

"What will that do?" Sharon asked, a valid question as she watched him move with practiced purpose.

So, Michael told her, *"Jack-o'-lanterns ward off evil spirits, making sure they can't pass the point at which they are*

61

placed, protecting your home or whatever is behind them. Well, in the same way, you can use them to trap evil ghosts from leaving a place. And the burning sage is for weakening magical practitioners like witches and warlocks. Wear this holly root, because with it, no magical practitioner can harm you with magic."

Michael educates her as he places a silver necklace around her neck, the heart locket cool against her skin, the holly root inside giving off a soft, earthy scent that makes the air feel a little safer.

"Why didn't you think of this before we got to the safe house, sir?" Sharon said, making a point.

"I was checking out your ass, sorry, OK, but at least I backtracked and got what was needed," Michael admitted, embarrassed.

"You better be telling me the truth this time, and was doing that and not checking out Cathy's," Sharon warned him, then moved toward the building to save her witness, with Mike following close behind.

Once inside, they saw hooded figures running scared. One warlock tried to use magic on them, but couldn't because of their silver necklaces with the holly root. When that didn't work, the warlock swung on Michael, but Michael moved out of the way and used his sharp machete, severing the forearm of the magical practitioner. The severed limb hit the floor with a dull slap, dark smoke rising from the wound as the warlock screamed.

Finding an unconscious Catherine, Michael picked her up and carried her to safety while Sharon kept them covered, her weapon steady, her pulse racing.

Arriving at the Heightened Hills Hospital, Catherine was admitted as a patient through the ER, the automatic doors hissing open as they rushed inside.

Chapter 10

It's All Hallows' Eve now. *"Happy Halloween,"* a nurse says to another one as Sharon looks on, the decorations in the hallway casting soft orange reflections across the sterile floor.

Michael comes back from talking with the doctor and informs Sharon, *"The doctor says Cathy will be fine. Once she received a blood transfusion, she's gonna make it."* Mike sounds relieved, the tension finally loosening from his shoulders after worrying so long.

"Do you still care about her?" Sharon asks, needing to know; her voice low and edged with something she can't quite hide.

"I swear it's just as a friend, nothing more," Michael reassures Sharon.

"I hope so, Tiger," Sharon says, genuine in her feelings. She continues, leaning in a little, *"What's next, Mike? How do we track down the criminals in your world?"* Her tone is flirtatiously curious as she waits for his answer.

"We go back to where we came from. Because of the Jack-o'-lanterns, the familiars that are connected to the warlocks and witches are trapped, and the coven won't abandon them. So, we will interrogate them and hopefully get some answers," Michael says, letting Sharon in on his ingenious plan.

However, Sharon had to ask, *"But won't the witches just remove the Jack-o'-lanterns for their spirit host?"* She feels it's a logical conclusion, and the worry shows in her eyes.

"Jack-o'-lanterns with something like sage burning in them is like introducing garlic to a vampire when dealing with anyone practicing dark magic. You get it now?" Mike reveals, his voice low and matter-of-fact, as if this is basic supernatural safety 101.

"Okay, let's go!" Sharon felt enthused, a spark of determination lighting up inside her.

As they arrive back at the scene of the sacrifice, they are met by the practitioners standing on the other side of a Jack-o'-lantern.

"So, the detective returns with the Wiccan," a practitioner of dark magic says sarcastically, then calls out to someone, *"Midnight! They're here."*

Next, the same beautiful young woman from Sheriff Krueger's home and the safe house emerges from the dark shadows and stands before Sharon and Michael. Her presence chills the air, the shadows almost clinging to her as if obeying her.

"You killed Waning Moon, our leader. I thought you Wiccans believed in 'harm you none,'" Midnight sneered at Michael, her voice sharp and cold.

"Actually, the proper quote is, 'An it harm none, do what ye will,'" Michael corrects her, then goes on. *"Your leader was trying to attack me, and I defended myself. Besides, his surname clearly defined his ultimate destiny anyway."* Michael reminds her how each magical name has a purpose.

Midnight, the coven's new leader now by default, acknowledges Michael's insight with a respectful nod. Then she responds, *"Though your point is valid, by you trapping us and enabling us not to use our magic with the burning sage, we could not heal him. So, in essence, you played a part in harming him."* Midnight feels the need to put a fine point on things.

"And that is where you grey practitioners get it all wrong, because most of you, from my experience, put too much emphasis on the magical properties of things, rather than using practical knowledge. Like taking off your belt, for example, and tying it just above the wound to slow the bleeding, and then cauterizing it." Michael educates her, his tone sharp but steady.

"What happens now, Wiccan?" Midnight asks, fed up with Michael at this point and just wanting to know where they go from here.

"Who is this blood queen... or king? No games, because I know you know." Michael demands, his voice lowering with intensity as he presses for the identity of the vampire leader.

"First things first, who's the Alpha of the Wolfpack?" Asks Midnight.

"Your guess is as good as mine. Now who's the vampire leader, or I'll leave y'all here to rot," Michael says, making it clear he isn't playing around.

Midnight thinks for a moment, then continues, *"Paris Hemingway."*

"You mean... Doctor Paris Hemingway?" Sharon asks, needing confirmation; her mind flashes back to the hospital. She had spoken to that woman. Stood in front of her. Looked

her in the eyes. There had been nothing, no hint, no shadow, no flicker of anything monstrous. Just a calm, professional doctor doing her job. Sharon's chest tightens. She could've never guessed that the woman she met earlier, the one surrounded by medical charts and sterile lighting, was actually a vampire… let alone a leader, a Blood Queen!

The betrayal of that normal façade rattles her more than she wants to admit.

"Yes," Midnight reveals.

And right there, Henry's words start making sense to Sharon. Henry wasn't talking crazy after all. Everything clicks; the patterns, the attacks, and now why the assault on the asylum is happening.

"Oh, God. Do you know where Dr. Hemingway is right now?!" Sharon says, the realization hits her like a punch to the chest.

"We were supposed to meet up at her home here in Heightened Hills after our… well, you stopped us from doing that, so I guess she's still waiting," Midnight sneered.

Michael lifts the Jack-o'-lantern and backs away, signaling Sharon to stay behind him. *"Go, attend to your dead in peace. Blessed Be,"* Michael says, giving his farewell. The coven does just that, retreating in silence.

Above them, the clouds begin to shift, slowly peeling away to reveal a Bloodmoon. Its red glow spills over the ground like a warning. Sharon, looking at the BloodMoon, feels the hair on her arms rising. Michael takes note of it too; all this is new to him, unsettling even. There's never been a

Bloodmoon Halloween before, and the sight leaves them both momentarily still.

"Hopefully it's a sign of ill fortune or change for our enemies and not us, if not, then self-reflection on all," Michael says, sharing his thoughts with Sharon as he studies the moon. Sharon struggles to understand, so Michael tells her, *"Never mind, let's just get to Hemingway's home."* Mike clearly wants to move on.

They hurry back to the car. Michael starts the engine, and the two of them take off down the road, the Bloodmoon hanging above them like a warning. Sharon keeps glancing at it through the windshield, feeling a pressure in her chest she cannot explain. The streets grow quieter the closer they get to Dr. Hemingway's neighborhood.

At the Hemingway house, Sharon and Michael walk up the front steps and knock. The porch light flickers. No answer. Michael pushes the door, testing it, and the lock gives way with a soft crack. They step inside cautiously.

As they walked in, they saw Dr. Hemingway standing alone in her living room, perfectly still, almost as if she had been waiting.

Sharon draws her gun. *"Unless that's silver bullets, you'll be able to do nothing,"* Paris laughs.

Mike takes out his crucifix. Hemingway backs up slightly and says, *"So..., you do have weapons."* Paris realizes she has underestimated them.

Moments later, they hear wolves howling outside the house. The sound vibrates through the walls and the floorboards. *"I may have lost the turf war, but you now have joined me in Schitt's Creek,"* Hemingway says in a schadenfreude tone.

Michael and Sharon look through the windows and see Jeff and Lucy, along with officers from both Heightened Hills and Social Falls, surrounding the house and standing with werewolves. Then, right before their eyes, those officers transform into Lycans too. Bones snap, silhouettes twist, and fur ripples over human skin. The sight freezes both Michael and Sharon.

"Take this, you're going to need it," Michael says, giving Sharon wolfsbane. Sharon notes that its color reminds her of Henry's jacket.

From the corner of her eye, Sharon noticed movement near the back hallway. A figure stepped forward, slow and deliberate. Cathy. Her hooded poncho shadowed most of her face, but even in the dim light, Sharon could see her eyes, colder, sharper, touched by something animal. She should not have been able to stand after what happened at the ritual site, but the bite from the werewolf had clearly done more than save her life. It had changed her. And she hadn't come alone. The faint scent of fur and earth clung to her like a second skin.

"Join us. Alpha will be merciful," Cathy says to them, her voice eerie and unfamiliar.

"I will never serve werewolves!" Hemingway said.

Just then, a Lycan walks in; its massive form filling the doorway. Sharon blurts out her thought without meaning to,

69

"Is this Alpha?" Her eyes had dropped instinctively between its legs before she could stop herself.

Cathy answers immediately, *"No, but I can recognize those balls from anywhere."* She cuts herself off, realizing what she just admitted.

The Lycan steps forward and transforms into a man, bones crackling, fur peeling back, muscles tightening. It's Henry… in full Monty. Sharon stares at him, stunned. He looks nothing like the broken, frantic man she'd seen in that asylum. This version of him is taller, harder, carved from muscle and something feral. Power rolls off him in waves, and for a moment, Sharon forgets to breathe. She can't help staring at his abs and the bare, unapologetic physicality of him; shock and disbelief tighten her throat.

"Who's gawking at who's man now, bitch!" Cathy taunts Sharon with a malicious grin, clearly enjoying the moment.

"Now, since I have your undivided attention, join us or die," Henry says to Michael and Sharon. His voice is calm, almost too calm, and that makes it worse.

Without warning, he shifts again, bones snapping and skin tearing as he becomes a Lycan in an instant. Cathy joins him, her own body contorting into a werewolf beside him. The two of them pounce on Hemingway before she can even react, dragging her across the floor and into the dining room.

Sharon hears the chair legs scraping. The thud of bodies hitting walls. Then the sound that makes her stomach twist, the wet, tearing munching. Flesh, cracking. Bones being pulled. Michael flinches at the noise as the feeding grows louder, the whole house echoing with the undeniable fact that Paris Hemingway is not coming back.

From the hallway came the soft shuffle of small feet, followed by a faint humming, that same eerie tune Sharon hears for the first time from Kiki. Shadows stretched across the doorway a moment before three figures emerged. Monica stepped in first, calm and collected as if she'd been waiting for this exact moment. Zack and Kiki trailed behind her, both wrapped in hooded ponchos that hid most of their expressions except their eyes, which gleamed with a feral hunger. They had come from the back of the house, drawn by the noise of the fight and the scent of blood drifting through the air. Monica paused in the entryway, surveying the chaos with unsettling ease, like she had been lurking just out of sight, listening, calculating, and had chosen this moment to reveal her true self.

"Now, who goes first?" Zack taunts the duo, eyes glinting with something far more feral than playful.

"I get first dibs on snacks, remember!" Kiki reminds him, sounding anxious and excited, like she's waiting for candy, not blood.

Next, Monica steps in behind them. *"Now, children, stop fighting,"* she says, stern but calm, like she's breaking up a squabble instead of walking into a slaughterhouse. The chewing continues in the dining room, wet and constant.

"Alpha," Sharon says, staring at Monica. Monica responds with a small curtsy, casual and chilling.

"So, you're the wolfpack Joseph was hunting," Michael says.

71

"Yes, and my husband saved us," Monica replies, as the sounds of gnawing keep echoing behind her.

"I won't go out like Joseph," Michael warns.

"I've killed many Shadow Hunters, so what's one more?" Monica says. Then she pulls her gun and fires. Michael drops hard, hitting the floor with a lifeless thud. Monica turns to the kids. *"Snack time,"* she says maliciously.

And the children feast.

Sharon struggles to stand, her legs shaking beneath her like they're made of wet paper. Her breath comes in sharp, ragged pulls as she forces herself upright. The wolfsbane burns cold in her palm, almost vibrating, its bitter scent flooding her nose. She lifts her weapon with her other trembling hand, the barrel wobbling as she tries to steady her aim. The house smells like copper, wet fur, and something rotten, and every sound, every chew, every drip, makes her stomach turn. Still, she fires.

"Good thing that's not silver bullets in your gun," Monica laughs it off after being shot. She returns the favor, firing twice, and the impact rips through Sharon's wrist and leg like fire eating through bone. Sharon's body jerks, her gun slipping from her fingers and skittering across the floor with a metallic clatter.

Monica steps over her like she's a rug. *"Look on the bright side, at least you're not a mother,"* she taunts, her voice dripping with malice.

Then Monica leans down and bites Sharon on the shoulder. The teeth sink in deep. Sharon feels the puncture before the pain, a cold shock followed by a brutal, burning pressure that spreads through her nerves like electricity. She hears the crunch of her own skin breaking, feels warm blood sliding down her arm, feels Monica's breath hot and animal against her neck.

Sharon's knees buckle, and her limbs grow impossibly heavy, like someone poured concrete into her veins. The room spins, the ceiling folding into the walls. Her heartbeat becomes a slow, distant drum. The last thing she feels is the cold floor rushing up to meet her.

Then everything goes black...

The end?